Gladys

Flash Harry

Martha

ALBERT

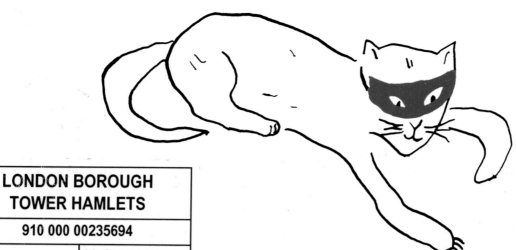

WHEN THE THE MICE

LIONEL

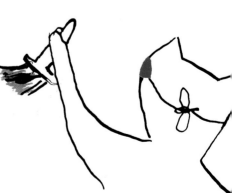

ALBERT

Audrey

ha

Flash Harry

Martha

MARTHA'S CATS AWAY WILL PLAY

Bruce Ingman

WALKER BOOKS
AND SUBSIDIARIES
LONDON · BOSTON · SYDNEY · AUCKLAND

When you go off to school,
you think I just sleep all day:

WELL, BOY,
HAVE I GOT NEWS
FOR YOU!

I have my own newspaper delivered to keep myself up to date with the goings-on in the cat world.

I keep myself fit to make sure that the dog next door can't catch me.

At ten o'clock I set up my easel
and paints and *Gladys* from
No. 34 pops round to pose for me.

I cook myself a spot of lunch: my favourite is a nice bit of salmon washed down with a cool saucer of milk.

I like to watch the cartoons
while I have my lunch.

I phone my cousin **ALBERT** in Skegness for a chat.

Sometimes in the afternoon Flash Harry knocks on the back door with his suitcase full of goodies.

I have a little nap and, WOW,
do I have some good dreams.

I listen to the radio. I like the gardening programmes that tell me all about the plants and flowers in our garden.

Then I go upstairs to get changed for my afternoon performance.

Cats come from far and near
to hear me play.

They are very
generous with their
applause and I usually
do a couple of encores.

I play with your toys. *Audrey* from across the road calls round quite often to play doctors and nurses.

If there's any time to spare, I take the car for a quick spin around your room.

When I hear the garden gate, I dash downstairs to the sofa and pretend to be in the Land of Nod. Then you rush into the room and kiss me hello, thinking I have been asleep all day.

Well, now you
know!

This book is especially for Jessie

First published 1995

This paperback edition published 2010 by Walker Books Ltd
87 Vauxhall Walk, London SE11 5HJ

2 4 6 8 10 9 7 5 3 1

© 1995 Bruce Ingman

The right of Bruce Ingman to be identified as author/illustrator of this work has been
asserted by him in accordance with the Copyright, Designs and Patents Act 1988

This book has been typeset in Caslon 224

Printed in China

British Library Cataloguing in Publication Data:
a catalogue record for this book is available from the British Library

ISBN 978-1-4063-2960-5

www.walker.co.uk

ALBERT

Audrey

ha

Flash Harry

Martha

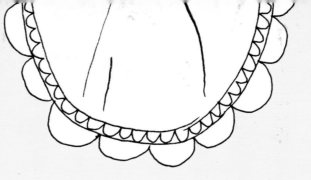
Flash Harry

Gladys

Martha

ALBERT

Another title by

Bruce Ingman

ISBN: 978-1-84428-456-6

"Story is usually, by definition, secondary to illustration,
but even very little ones appreciate a good narrative ...
Bad News, I'm in Charge! expertly combines the two."
Observer

"Ingman's pictures tell the story entirely from a child's perspective,
allowing readers to reach their own conclusions."
Guardian

Available from all good bookstores

www.walker.co.uk